Adventure stories for kids.

'All Year through for Cute You!'

Second edition

Author: Volha Melgaard

Illustrator: Abishan Ashley

To memory of my Mom, who brought the warm-hearted world emotions and feelings to my childhood.

Blossom Spring is new beginning.

Once a year when the gardens bloom, the little fairies, boys, and girls, appear from inside the flowers. They have small wings that sparkle in the darkness. Fairies are magical creatures, but they can only be seen by small children. Fairies fly from flower to flower and can even fly inside the houses of obedient kids to tell them a bedtime story.

And when the gardens wither, fairies turn into stars and fly back to the sky.

Inside a blooming garden runs a little boy, Kirill. He was catching butterflies when he accidentally caught a small fairy.

"Let me go, please," asks the Fairy.

"Oh, no!" Kirill is indignant. "I will show you to my mum and dad!" He ran with all his force back to his house.

"Mummy, Mummy! Look what I have caught!"

Mum looks inside his butterfly ring-net and can see nothing, because adults cannot see fairies.

"The child imagines things," thinks Mum and, in order not to offend him, gently adds, "It is very interesting! Show it to your Daddy."

"Daddy, Daddy!" shouts Kirill joyfully. "Look what I caught!"

Dad looks into a butterfly ring-net and, of course, can see nothing.

"Very interesting!" says Dad, who did not want to upse his kid. Then he jokes, "Show it to Borman. He would like it!"

He meant a large, ginger cat called Borman, wh sometimes lives in a house with Kirill, and other times in th garden on his own.

"Look, Borman, what a wonderful butterfly!" shouts th kid loudly, right into the cat's ear, putting the butterfly ring net under the cat's nose.

"If I were in your place, I would let this butterfly- fairy g before something bad happens!" meows the cat wisely.

Kirill slumps down on his bottom, "How can my cat ta with a human voice?"

"Let me go, Kirill, please!" pleads the Fairy again. "I hav already granted you an ability to understand all the languag of the world in exchange for my freedom!"

"No, no, no!" refuses the boy bluntly. "I will show you all my friends!" And his eyes lit up with the mischievous fire a naughty boy when he imagines how surprised they wou be.

"Well, blame yourself then!" the Fairy loses her temp and turns purple with rage. Her little wings convert themselv into huge and sharp, which easily cut the net. She is nc above the boy's head, and says, "And now you will become small that you would be frightened even of a Ladybird!"

And before Kirill could understand what Fairy was saying, he falls on something fluffy and ginger.

"Be careful!" shouts angry Borman. Kirill's size was reduced to the size of the Fairy and the boy fell right on cat back. "Mm, my friend, you are in a big trouble. Plea forgiveness from the Fairy on the spot!"

But it was too late. The purple Fairy-butterfly with "shar wings" had already disappeared behind the trees.

Kirill looks around. The trees, the bushes, and even th grass all become so huge. The huge eyes of Borman look a him compassionately and his huge mouth meows

"Okay, I will help you to find the Fairy, as you often three me pieces of chicken under the table during dinner!" And h hobbles lazily into the garden with Kirill on his back.

The Cat sniffs the grass, sniffs the air, and strides straig to the apple tree. There, among the foliage in the huge app tree blossoms, sits many cheerful fairies. Kirill would nev have noticed them if he was not so small.

"Look, a novice!" chirps some fairies cheerfully, flocking around Kirill. "And where did you leave your wing We will find you the new ones!"

The boy did not manage to mutter a word, as they glu wonderful wings onto his back. Kirill tried it and flew! High and higher above the grass, on and on the top of the app tree.

It had been a long time ago since Kirill had enjoyed imself to such an extent. He imagines himself as an airplane overing with a buzz between the huge pink and white ragrant flowers of the apple tree.

"Oh!" the cat thinks. "If he flies away, who will provide ne with the tasty bits under the table?"

He shouts, "Wait a minute! This is not a fairy-boy! He is ן ordinary boy who was turned into a dwarf by the Fairy ecause he did not want to let her go. We came to apologize!"

All the fairies freeze. Kirill notices a huge black cloud overing the garden with threatening shadow. It is the shadow f the purple Fairy, who scattered her wings right over his ead.

"I am…I am sorry, I will never do anything like that again!" rill whimpers, stuttering of fear.

"I might forgive you," says the purple Fairy less angrily, "if vitness that you really did repent yourself and you will never ;ain bully those who are smaller and weaker than you."

The boy sobs again and starts walking inside the garden. ıddenly, there is a large 'meow' from Borman. The cat anages to jump up and catch the purple Fairy in flight. He esses her heftily down to the ground and hisses, nmediately turn Kirill back into a big boy! It is our dinner on and we don't have time to seek your forgiveness!"

"Let her go!" sobs Kirill, turning back. "I blame only yself. I must put everything right. I must stop bullying those smaller and weaker than me!" To his amazement, the cat let the butterfly go. The purple butterfly turns herself into sparkling and kind Fairy because she was so touched by the boy's words. Other fairies fly to her and together, after some whispering, they burst out laughing.

Kirill begins to grow at an astounding speed. He even feels that he could have touched the clouds.

"Oh, here are you, my boy!" He returns to reality by the sound of his mother's voice. "It's dinner time. Don't forgot to wash your hands with soap."

Kirill looks around. There are no fairies, no wings on his back. Only Borman proudly converting his tail into a pipe shape and happily rubbing it against the boy's leg.

"Was it only my imagination?" Kirill asks, happy that he got back his normal size.

"Well, let's go home quickly and have our dinner," he said loudly to Borman. The cat only meows in return, not with human voice anymore.

After his dinner, Kirill puts away the ring-net for catching butterflies in a very secret place, just in case.

THE END

Hot Summer Will Show.

It was long hot summer. A little boy, Sasha, lived on th shore. He often walked by the water, collecting seashells, an throwing little stones into the incoming waves.

There was a lonely Mermaid living in the big, blue sea. A day long, she would look at the shore with her huge, sad ey and sing sad songs.

"Ah!" the Mermaid thought one day, "I wish I could gr the little boy by his tiny foot and drag him into cold sea wi me forever. Then, I wouldn't be so lonely and sad anymore.

She swam quietly to the little boy and smiled. Sash surprised, threw a seashell at her.

"What are you?" he asked.

"I am a Mermaid! Swim with me to the sea! We will ri the waves and chase the seahorses, play hide-and-seek amo the reefs, and make friends with the jellyfish."

"Great!" Sasha clapped his hands with excitement a started to laugh.

The Mermaid put the boy on her shoulders and swa into the sea.

"Look, dolphins!" Sasha shouted as the dolphins chas each other. The huge sharks started to circle around them. B the Mermaid frowned angrily at them and they could only

chatter their teeth with frustration, because she woul
not allow to grab the little boy.

Suddenly, Sasha began to cry, "I want my mum!"

"What?" the Mermaid said with surprise. "But we ar
having so much fun together!"

"I want my mum!" The little tot burst into tears.

"You are probably hungry," guessed the Mermaid ar
gave him a sea lollipop. But it did not help for long, as the bc
began to cry again.

"I won't let you go!" The Mermaid became angry. "I a
your mum now, and if you cry any longer, I'll give you to th
sharks!"

Sasha stopped crying but no matter what the Merma
did for him, it was not fun anymore. The Mermaid had starte
to love the little boy. Now when he looked incredibly sad, sl
was ready to give away the whole underwater kingdom for h
laughter and to restore the happiness to his eyes.

The Mermaid put him on her shoulders again and th
swam to the huge turtle for advice.

"Hmm!" the turtle said meaningfully, with a sniff. "Gi
the boy back to his mum, while it is not too late! In a couple
days, he will turn into a mermaid and will stay forever lone
and sad in the sea, just like you!"

"Oh no!" the Mermaid exclaim. "To lose him now whe
have found my amusement and happiness! No, no! Never!"

"Mummy," Sasha cried louder and louder. He began t
turn blue with cold and did not want to have fun anymore.

Something burst in the Mermaid's chest. With a flick
her tail, they appeared on the shore near the little boy's hom
He screamed very loudly, "Mummy!"

The Mermaid hugged and kissed Sasha for the last tim
and disappeared back into the cold sea.

The shore was in a commotion! There were happy cri
from his mother and the sound of her child's laughter.

For some reason, the Mermaid felt warm and calm inside ar
the sea did not seem as cold anymore. The Mermaid began
sing happily and peacefully for the first time in her life.

THE END

The Mystery of Autumn.

There is old castle in the woods among the bushes o jasmine and lilac. Anna and her little brother Michael live there. The castle's huge mosaic windows are magical. On a sunny day when colourful patches of sunlight are playing across the rooms, soft and pleasant music can be heard al around.

On a rainy day, Anna and Michael love to sit and watch the fire in a large fireplace. It is raining and windy outside, bu warm and cosy by the fire. This brother and sister always loo forward to the autumn rain because a kind, old lady ofter comes to visit them on such days. Her clothes are alway sopping wet and never dry out no matter how long she sits b the fireplace. Her hair is bright red, like autumn leaves. Ann says that it is Autumn herself who comes to visit their ol castle for a cup of tea and to warm herself up by the fire. Th old lady always tells the children fascinating tales.

Today, she begins her story in a peculiarly pensiv manner.

"Once upon a time when Autumn was a young, rec haired girl," she starts. "She loved to lark in th neighbourhood. One day, she filled all the roads with faller red leaves so no one could get by. Another day, she sent suc a strong wind and hailstorm to surrounding villages where th

people had to stay indoors for days. People began complaining to the Sun.

"Oh the Great Eye of Day! Every year, you send Autumn, Winter, Spring, and Summer to the Earth. Please stop this mischievous autumn! We will be so happy without her: there will be neither annoying, cold rain, nor nasty mud on the roads!"

The Sun smiled and said, "Fine, people, I will do what you want. I forbid Autumn from coming to earth anymore! But remember, if you want her to come back again, she will have to lose her youth and beauty!"

The people just laughed in response.

"Thankfully, Autumn will never want to come back from now on!"

Autumn disappeared and the Winter began, full of fun with its snow and frost. Then, there was the beautiful Spring with its flowers and singing birds. After Spring, there was a hot Summer with bright sunshine and fine days. The people were happy because they had gotten rid of Autumn's foul weather. To their displeasure though, Summer wouldn't finish. Instead, Summer would start over and over again like a stuck record. There weren't any flowers, greenery, or bountiful harvest anymore. Everything was burnt by the heat. People began to wail and cry. They realized that without Autumn, there would be no Winter or Spring or a nice Summer again. They had disrupted the natural cycle of time. People started calling to

Autumn, begging her to come back. They promised her "We will make bonfires, sing and dance in your honour, we wi praise your rich crops and unique beauty of your nature!''

By that time, Autumn was very bored and tired of he loneliness and isolation. She was looking forward to paintin the trees red, pouring on the ground with rain, driving gre clouds, and enjoying a rich harvest.

Autumn came back to Earth not a young girl anymore, bu an old lady. When Autumn cries for her lost youth, it ca sometimes feel so sad on rainy evenings.

The old lady finishes her story and wipes away a tea Then, she cheerfully claps her hands and lots of tasty foo appear on the table. The children immediately forget her stor and gladly tuck into the delicious treats.

Autumn watches them and thinks, "It doesn't matte whether you are young or old. If you have everything in you life or just very little of what you wish. It's more important tha you are able to enjoy your life, the same as children ca appreciate every little treat they get! Then, even on a du rainy day, your heart will be filled with joy and happiness.

THE END

A

Christmas Gift for a Kid.

The little boy called Lee looked out of his window. It was snowing and the fluffy snowflakes were quietly covering the roofs of the houses, the trees, and the square where the big Christmas tree stood. The old tower clock struck midnight and Lee suddenly felt that something was about to happen. At the beginning, he heard the clip-clop of hooves. There were some golden reindeer flying in the sky hauling a huge, magic sleigh. In the sleigh, there were toys, that were singing and dancing. The golden reindeer and the magic sleigh flew around the Christmas tree a few times. Suddenly, the Christmas tree began to grow and grow, right up to the sky!

"I wish I could ride in the sleigh with those toys!" Lee thought, and he closed his eyes tightly with delight when he imagined himself in the magic sleigh. When he opened his eyes, he saw a chocolate bear and a lollipop in the shape of birdie next to him!

"What is this? How is that possible?" He was racing with the toys in the magic sleigh around the Christmas tree! The huge, silver balls and glittering garlands were flying toward him from the opposite direction. Everywhere on the Christmas tree the crackers exploded, and a colourful rain of sweets and chocolates poured onto Lee's head. He caught a few sweets but did not even have time to open the wrapping when the sleigh stopped next the Christmas tree. There, under a shining

star, a party table was set with a huge cake in the middle The cake was like a snow-white, sugar castle.

All the other guests were already there: teddy bears, gnomes, dolls. Toy planes and helicopters were flying over the table, and toy trains and cars were buzzing around. Little, gold angels blew trumpets and the Blizzard-maid appeared in the sky. She waved her magic wand to the right and left, and fluffy white snowflakes began to dance around the Christmas tree. One of the snowflakes picked up Lee and together, they flew to the top of the cake. Lee poked through the sugar roof of the sweet castle and fell in.

Wow! So delicious were the castle's walls and windows!

Suddenly, the sugar castle began to disappear as the guests began taking the cake apart piece by piece. The teddy bear got the biggest slice, and the birdie got the smallest one.

The gold angels began to treat the guests with the Blizzard-maid's cocktail. It was warm milk with honey and cinnamon, sprinkled with chocolate. The Blizzard-maid was sitting on an ice throne at the head of the table and was looking at everyone with a little surprise in her glance.

Suddenly, someone shouted, "Ho! Ho! Ho! Who dare take my sleigh without my permission?"

It was Santa Claus! He sat down on the ice throne at the other end of the table opposite the Blizzard-maid. He could not catch his breath. All this time, he had been chasing the magic sleigh around the sky. Everything turned quiet. All the

naughty toys hid under the table. Only Lee remained sitting. He was choking with excitement.

"I rode but only a little bit," he finally said.

"Enough, Santa Claus, you're scaring our guests!" the Blizzard-maid said and began to laugh. "It's your own fault. You slept and missed your sleigh. Because of you, the toys were nearly late for the Christmas party!" Then she calmingly added with a cheeky wink, "Please, try my cocktail and take the presents out of your magic sleigh. Can't you see we have little Lee here? He was a good boy all year and deserves the present of his dream!"

After drinking the Blizzard-maid's cocktail, Santa Claus mellowed and rolled open his very long list of presents. All the toys came out from under the table and began to wait with curiosity,

wondering what present Lee would get. And the little boy really wished that Santa Claus would present him with new bicycle!

Suddenly the old tower clock struck again, and Lee woke up. He sat upright on the bed, frustrated: how could he wake up at such an important moment? The giving of presents! Lee dashed to the window and on the way, caught his foot on something in the dark. Something very familiar clanked and made his heart pound. He opened the curtains and in the light of early morning, he saw a new, blue bicycle with a wonderful ilver horn in his room! The present stood by the window, calling out to be taken for a ride!

"It's so great that Santa Claus guessed what I wanted!" exclaimed Lee.

The Christmas lights, like the stars, started to become invisible in the daylight. And the whole world was absorbed by quiet Christmas morning!

THE END

Dear friend,

Thank you for choosing to read my book. I really appreciate it and am happy to share my fantasy word of magical adventures with you. I hope you enjoyed m stories and I'm looking forward to entertaining you again and again.

This is my first book. A such, I would love to know wha you think about my fairy tales so I can improve them i the future.

If you have a moment, my dear friend, could you please do me the honor of providing an honest opinion: were my stories touching and which was you favorite?

Thank you very much for your time and I wish you success and happiness!

Sincerely,

Volha Melgaard

Printed in Great Britain
by Amazon